FORTY-HOUR RUNATHON

Pat Quinn

CONTENTS

photographs by David Hamilton

🍃 Learning Media®

THE CHALLENGE

Each year, the students at James Sanders High School hold a fundraiser for a **charity**. Recently, they challenged themselves to raise $50,000 for World Vision in a forty-hour runathon.

APRIL   MAY   JUNE   JULY

The students challenge themselves to raise
$50,000 during a forty-hour runathon.

Every year, World Vision (which is one of the largest aid organizations in the world) holds an event in which people are sponsored to go without food for thirty or forty hours. Besides raising money for World Vision, participants get an idea of what it feels like to be really hungry. Instead of not eating, the students at James Sanders High School decided to challenge themselves to run for forty hours. The money they raised would be used in countries that have been devastated by war, drought, or famine.

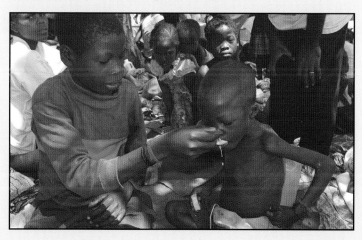

AUGUST   SEPTEMBER   OCTOBER   NOVEMBER

THE PLAN

Six months before the runathon, a group of students met to begin planning the event. They came up with two objectives:

1. To raise $50,000 in a nonstop forty-hour run around Wilmore Park, starting at 6 a.m. on Thursday and finishing at 10 p.m. on Friday;

2. To work together as a team.

APRIL   MAY   JUNE   JULY

The students meet to begin planning the runathon.

*To raise **$50,000** in a nonstop forty-hour run around Wilmore Park, starting at 6 a.m. on Thursday and finishing at 10 p.m. on Friday*

The students had organized fundraising events before, so they knew that their idea could work. Each runner would ask friends and family to be **sponsors**, paying a small amount for each lap the runner completed. After many, many laps, these small amounts would add up!

To help reach the $50,000 target, the students thought of several other ways to raise money:

1. Students could collect donations from bystanders during the runathon.

2. Local businesses could be asked to sponsor a team, and their name or product would be displayed on the day of the run.

AUGUST   SEPTEMBER   OCTOBER   NOVEMBER

The students' second idea required some thought. They were aware that people often wrote to businesses asking for sponsorship and that these letters often ended up in the trash, so they needed to ask for support in an interesting and a creative way.

The students decided to give potential sponsors a bucket that contained boxes of juice.

" It's like saying 'Here's some juice, and here's how you can help us provide juice for the rest of the world.'"

DENISE

James Sanders High
World Vision Runathon

APRIL   MAY   JUNE   JULY

The students decide to give potential sponsors a bucket that explains the runathon.

Each box of juice would be labeled with ways that money could be donated:

1. You could pay $1,000 to sponsor a team. Each team member will wear a T-shirt displaying your company's name.

2. You could donate a prize, such as a company product, for students who do well during the forty-hour runathon.

3. You could make a donation to World Vision.

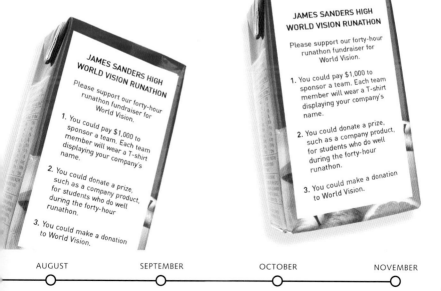

JAMES SANDERS HIGH
WORLD VISION RUNATHON

Please support our forty-hour runathon fundraiser for World Vision.

1. You could pay $1,000 to sponsor a team. Each team member will wear a T-shirt displaying your company's name.

2. You could donate a prize, such as a company product, for students who do well during the forty-hour runathon.

3. You could make a donation to World Vision.

JAMES SANDERS HIGH
WORLD VISION RUNATHON

Please support our forty-hour runathon fundraiser for World Vision.

1. You could pay $1,000 to sponsor a team. Each team member will wear a T-shirt displaying your company's name.

2. You could donate a prize, such as a company product, for students who do well during the forty-hour runathon.

3. You could make a donation to World Vision.

AUGUST   SEPTEMBER   OCTOBER   NOVEMBER

OBJECTIVE TWO

To work together as a team

Five students volunteered to mastermind the plan. They were known as the Top Five.

THE TOP FIVE

Each member of the Top Five headed a **committee** that took responsibility for one of five main areas:

1. Coordinating all the events associated with the forty-hour run

2. Promoting the event and organizing media coverage, for example, contacting newspapers and radio and TV stations

3. Taking care of the money

4. Managing the teams

5. Overseeing the entire project

| Johnny | Denise | Ryan | Nicola | Vince |

APRIL   MAY   JUNE   JULY

The Top Five meet for three days of planning.

During the summer vacation, the Top Five met for three days of intensive planning. They identified potential sponsors and organized the buckets. Then they started calling businesses.

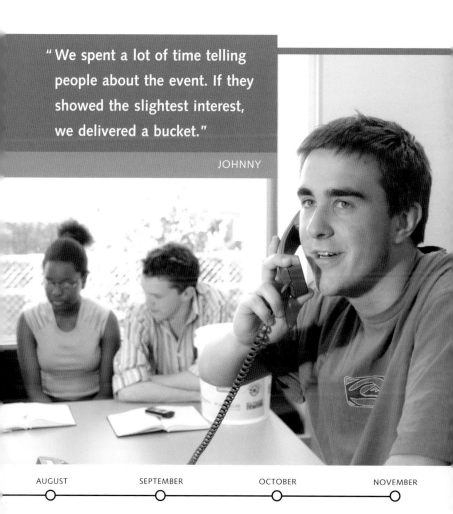

"We spent a lot of time telling people about the event. If they showed the slightest interest, we delivered a bucket."

JOHNNY

AUGUST   SEPTEMBER   OCTOBER   NOVEMBER

THE PREPARATION

When the new school year began, ten businesses had each agreed to sponsor a team. The school was divided into ten teams, and each team was allocated a sponsor. Every team had about a hundred students of all ages.

The Top Five gave the teams a running schedule, and several of the older students were responsible for making sure that people ran at the right times. The schedule allowed fifteen minutes per runner, with some team members running more than once.

APRIL   MAY   JUNE   JULY

Another local high school decided that it would like to be involved, and it entered a team. The Top Five decided to organize the run as a competition to encourage students to take part. The team that did the most laps during the forty hours would be the winner.

Each runner would wear a T-shirt with their sponsor's name printed on the back. Ten T-shirts were allocated to each team, and the teams aimed to have a maximum of ten students running at the same time. When a runner's time was up, they'd give their T-shirt to the person who was running next.

To keep the event fun for those waiting to run, the Top Five organized a variety of games, races, crazy contests, and movies.

"Before the run even started, there was a great competitive spirit between the teams, which encouraged lots of people to sign up."

NICOLA

THE RUNATHON

The day before the race, a village of tents, where the students could eat, sleep, chat, and watch movies when they weren't running, was set up inside Wilmore Park. The sidewalk around the park was to be used as the running track, and students would be posted at various points along the way to collect money from bystanders.

The day of the run dawned hot and sunny, and the first runners set off at 6 a.m. The good weather and festive atmosphere in the park attracted a lot of spectators. The school band played, and some dance groups performed. There were other events, too, such as three-legged races, speed races, and an egg-in-the-mouth race. Visitors included local celebrities (some of whom even ran a lap of the course), newspaper and radio reporters, and TV crews. Everyone got into it!

APRIL   MAY   JUNE   JULY

After forty hours, the runathon ended at 10 p.m. on Friday night.

"The atmosphere at the park was really cool – you could hang out in the park and play games or watch movies."

VINCE

AUGUST   SEPTEMBER   OCTOBER   NOVEMBER

The runathon is held.

THE RESULT

Everyone had a great time! Each runner averaged ten laps during their fifteen-minute run, and one student ran a total of one hundred and seventy laps – that's around 90 miles (145 kilometers). The runners covered about 12,000 miles (19,000 kilometers) in total.

Best of all, the total collected was almost $44,000! Not quite the $50,000 the school had aimed for but a great result.

APRIL   MAY   JUNE   JULY

The school decided that it would definitely do a runathon again, and a few months later, the Top Five passed on their skills and knowledge to the group of students who would be in charge of the next runathon.

"We told them the most important thing of all was to make it fun!"

RYAN

AUGUST   SEPTEMBER   OCTOBER   NOVEMBER

A **debrief** is held.

GLOSSARY

charity: an organization that helps people

committee: a group of people who have a common goal

debrief: a meeting to discuss how successful something was

sponsor: a person or group who agrees to pay a certain sum of money to another person or group if they complete a particular task

INDEX

AUTHOR

Susan Paris

Jason sure had a mighty challenge. At the moment, the biggest challenge in my life is riding my bike to work in the wind. Some days it's so windy, I'm nearly blown back the way I came.

ILLUSTRATOR

Brian Harrison

I've illustrated many books for children, and I especially enjoy working on myths. Greece has always interested me – I've traveled there three times. I hope you enjoy this myth. There are all kinds of stories about ancient civilizations to discover and read.

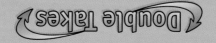

AUTHOR

Pat Quinn

At first, I thought that all a runathon involved was people running around a park for a certain length of time. When I wrote this book, I learned about the organization, teamwork, and effort involved in planning such an event.

PHOTOGRAPHER

David Hamilton

David Hamilton didn't pick up a camera until he was twenty-five! He's spent the last twenty years working as a photographer. He loves taking photos of people and exotic places. His work has taken him to Asia, South America, and Europe.

JASON
AND THE
GOLDEN FLEECE

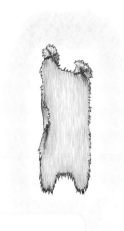

Susan Paris
illustrated by Brian Harrison

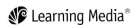 Learning Media®

Long ago in Greece, there lived a young man named Jason who was the son of a king. The king had a brother, Pelias, who had always been jealous of him. Pelias plotted against his brother, eventually forcing him from the throne.

Jason and his father fled to a mountain cave, where they met Chiron, a wise centaur. Chiron began teaching Jason to become a great warrior. Every night, Jason dreamed of winning back his father's kingdom.

After many months, Jason was ready to confront his uncle. Pelias had been warned that his nephew was coming and was waiting for him at the city gates.

"Welcome, Jason," he said with a broad smile. "You must be hungry after your long journey. Come and eat with me." Jason went with his uncle to the palace, where he ate an enormous meal before falling into a warm, comfortable bed.

The next morning, Pelias made Jason an offer. "If you travel to Colchis and bring me the golden fleece, I'll leave this city, and your father can return as king."

Chiron had told Jason many stories about the golden fleece. It hung from the branch of a huge tree near the city of Colchis and could be seen for miles around, casting its golden light across the land. The fleece was guarded by a dragon that never slept, and many people had died trying to claim it. Pelias believed it was an impossible challenge and his nephew would never return. Then he could rule the city in peace.

5

Jason knew it would be a difficult task. No one had ever managed to outwit the dragon, but he was determined to try and began to make plans right away. That afternoon, Jason visited Argus, the great shipbuilder. He realized it would be foolish to attempt such a long and difficult journey on his own, so he asked Argus to build a ship large enough to carry fifty men and strong enough to sail across the wild Black Sea.

Argus and his carpenters worked day and night. They built the ship's hull from the trunks of enormous oaks, then they carved oars, which would help the crew row safely past the many rocky coastlines and sandbars. Finally, Argus and his men sewed enormous sails to catch the ocean breeze.

While the ship was being built, Jason
instructed the city's messengers to travel
throughout Greece, spreading his plea for
help. Princes and noblemen came from far
and wide, including Orpheus, the musician.
They gathered on the beach in the shadow
of the great ship, which Argus had called *Argo*.

"We will sail to Colchis to claim the golden
fleece," Jason told them. "Nothing will stand
in the way of us – the fearless Argonauts." The
men cheered. Many of them dreaded tyrants
like Pelias and wanted to help overthrow him.
While Orpheus played his lyre, the men
dragged the *Argo* down to the ocean.

The Argonauts sailed north. They struck fierce storms and thick fog, and the journey was slow. After many days, they reached the Clashers – huge rocks that crushed anything that tried to pass between them. It seemed unlikely that they would ever get through, and Jason's heart was heavy. He had led his brave men into danger.

At dusk, Jason saw a dove hovering above the ship. It circled around them, then darted between the Clashers just before they slammed shut. "Quick!" Jason shouted to his crew. "Row as hard as you can." Together, they strained on the oars, and the *Argo* surged through the gap as the Clashers opened again.

Finally, the city of Colchis appeared on the horizon, and the Argonauts rowed for its shores. Although the king of Colchis appeared pleased to see them, he was secretly angry. He realized that Jason wanted the golden fleece and decided to make things difficult for him.

"You may attempt to take the golden fleece if you complete one small task," the king said. He instructed Jason to catch his fire-breathing bulls and use them to plow a field. Then Jason was to sow the field with the teeth of a dragon.

That evening, Jason sat in the palace garden. He knew he had little chance of completing the king's challenge and was filled with despair. As he rose to leave, a messenger came into the garden. The king's daughter, Medea, had seen Jason and wanted to help. Jason followed the messenger through the castle to Medea's chamber.

"If you trust me and do as the king says," Medea said, "you'll be successful." She gave Jason a basket of dragon's teeth and some ointment. "Rub the ointment over your body. It will make you as strong as seven men, and neither the sword nor fire will harm you." Before he left, Jason promised that if he were successful, he would make Medea his wife.

The next morning, Jason carried out the king's instructions. The ointment Medea had given him prevented the fire-breathing bulls from harming him. But, as he stood admiring the newly plowed field, the dragon's teeth turned into soldiers who began waving long swords.

"Give them the basket that held the teeth," Medea yelled. Jason threw the basket to the soldiers, and they began to fight one another until they had all been killed.

"Well done," said the king through his clenched teeth. "Maybe soon, the golden fleece will be yours."

That afternoon, Medea secretly visited Jason. "My father is plotting to kill you. We must get the golden fleece tonight and leave." She told Jason to find Orpheus, then they all hurried to the huge tree where the fleece hung.

The dragon was hideous – even in the soft golden light from the fleece. "Quick – play your lyre," Medea instructed Orpheus. The air was filled with the sound of soft music, and the dragon was soon lulled into a deep trance. Jason quietly stepped past the dragon and gently unhooked the fleece.

"Hurry," Medea hissed. "The dragon's waking." They all rushed toward the beach. The Argonauts, who had seen them coming, pulled up the ship's anchor.

Meanwhile, the dragon's angry roars had woken the king. He called for his sword and commanded his soldiers to stop the *Argo* from sailing. But it was too late. By the time they had reached the water, the Argonauts were rowing with all their might. The soldiers' arrows cut through the air but hit the ocean harmlessly with a soft patter like rain.

Onboard the *Argo*, the crew were overjoyed. Orpheus played a song of thanks, and they set sail for home. On his return, Jason presented the golden fleece to Pelias. As promised, his uncle left the city, never to return.